GRIND

And Other Strange Stories

Frank Theodat

Contents

Dedication	3
Introduction	5
Head Count	7
Feast	15
Illuminatus For a Penny-a-Word	35
Quota	51
Grind	63
Acknowledgements	79
About the Author	81

To Michelle

For her endless love, support, and encouragement

Introduction

In this collection, you will find five strange tales. Each story delves into the shadowy corners of a world dominated by corporations and examines the impact of such a setting on its inhabitants.

These are stories of Corpo Dread.

Inspired by the works of Rod Serling, Harlan Ellison, Charles Beaumont, Ray Bradbury, and Richard Matheson, this collection serves as a testament to fantasy's ability not only to entertain—which remains my ultimate goal—but also, as Harlan Ellison aptly put it, to "illuminate the human condition."

Much like Kafka used surrealist fantasy to depict the absurdity of being a cog in an oppressive bureaucratic machine, I employ these stories to spotlight the darker facets of corporate life, sometimes weaving allegories and, at other times, crafting cautionary tales.

I hope you enjoy these stories as much as I enjoyed writing them.

Frank Theodat

Head Count

Pushing through the glass revolving doors of Bronson, Stanley, Graf & Company, twenty-five year old Jeffrey Morenz struggled to carry his gym bag.

Three days had passed. His rain coat was caked in bile, blood, and the filth of the city.

His work boots left muddy foot prints on the otherwise pristine floors of the corporate high rise.

The young woman at reception began to gag as Jeffrey approached.

He slammed the gym bag on the desk. "I'm here to see Mr. Bronson," Jeffrey said, trying to keep himself from collapsing due to his exhaustion.

The poor woman belched and expelled bits of her lunch in the waste basket next to her. Soon the lobby became flooded with the reek of the bag.

"Name?" she squeaked

"Jeff Morenz. I'm here for my interview."

She picked up the phone, keeping a hand over her nose and mouth.

She muttered in an uneasy tone of voice, "Jeff Morenz is here to see you, sir." She listened. "Yes sir, his third interview." She put down the phone. "Go on up," she said, then coughed. "Level 12. Executive Boardroom."

Jeffrey threw the bag over his shoulder and trekked to the elevator.

Inside, he turned and watched the city lights through the glass as he ascended to the top floor. Normally he'd be home, walking with Tia, his fiance, in the cold, wet night.

But things were different now.

The economy had gone south. He lost his income, his apartment, his girlfriend, and whatever moral virtue he had left in him. Everything he once owned was sold at auction, though it made no difference. Work opportunities were drying up, and only a few of the larger firms were open to hiring. Eight months of rejections and failed interviews were enough to make any penniless man desperate.

He needed something, anything, to bring him back to his normal life. As the chimes rang with each passing floor, Jeffrey took a deep, long breath and stared at the gym bag. Funny, he had always considered himself a pacifist, one who would speak out against violence and thought himself above such vile behavior. But when times are tough, when food, housing, and jobs are scarce, a man's thoughts center only on his own survival.

Level 12.

The doors opened. Jeffrey took his bag and marched forward, walking through the opulent hallway in the Southern Gothic tradition complete with decorative displays of animal heads encased in gold.

He stopped at the mahogany double doors, knocked three times, and waited. The seconds felt like a lifetime, but soon the doors opened. Walking into the darkly lit room, Jeffrey was met by the partners, Mr. Stanley and Mr. Graf. They were seated in plush leather chairs at the far end of a conference table. In the back near a bar, an older man, maybe in his late 60s and dressed in a sharkskin gray vest and trousers, a crisp white shirt, and a regal magenta tie poured himself another glass of bourbon.

Jeffrey nearly collapsed at the near end of the table.

The old man in gray turned and looked. "Well, I'll be damned." He smiled. He carried a southern gentlemanly air about him.

"I'm here for the interview, Mr. Bronson"

"Take a seat, my boy! Seems like you've earned it." Bronson's voice was baked in Tennessee sunshine.

Jeffrey sat in the leather chair by his side and pulled the gym bag up on the table.

The old man said, "Drink?"

"Water. Please."

A quick snap of the old man's fingers, and a large glass pitcher of water appeared at the near end of the table. Jeffrey grabbed the pitcher with both hands and drank as much as he could.

"Something to eat?"

Jeffrey wanted to say "Yes sir," but he only nodded.

Mr. Bronson whistled and a half-rack of pork ribs, warm, smoky and dripping in barbecue sauce materialized before Jeffrey.

He was hungry. He couldn't stuff his face fast enough.

The older men laughed as they watched this sad display.

Mr. Stanley leaned forward and smiled. "Well fellas—" the portly partner's voice was thick and guttural. "What do we think young Jeffrey has brought us in the bag?" He rubbed his pudgy, sweaty hands together in such delight.

"Smells ripe to me," Mr. Graf said. He sat back in his chair with a nasally voice and rat-like face, and took in the foul aroma with great pleasure. His eyes were hidden behind dark oval glasses. He smiled, showing off his set of golden teeth.

"Well Jeff," Mr. Bronson said, "what's in the bag?"

With his sauce-covered fingers, Jeffrey pulled down the bag's zipper. He turned the bag up and emptied it.

Four heads rolled onto the conference table.

The eyes fell out of their orbital sockets. Four rotting green faces, three men and one former blonde.

Mr. Stanley and Mr. Graf rose to their feet with a roaring cheer and applause.

"My my," Mr. Bronson said. "You actually delivered. Well done, Jeffrey! I admit I'm surprised. The others candidates shied away from such a task."

Mr. Graf laughed. "Not afraid of a little blood sport, eh?" He caressed one of the decomposed heads.

Jeffrey stood up, still a bit unsteady. "I did what you asked. Do I get the job?"

Bronson smiled. "Well Jeffrey, this does make for a marvelous offering. Bringing us the heads of the other candidates is quite creative. Quite creative indeed.

"Well?" Jeffrey clutched at the empty, soiled bag.

An obscure whisper in a strange tongue trembled through the room.

Mr. Bronson nodded in agreement.

"Unfortunately, the firm is also going through cuts. Bad times, I'm afraid. But good luck in your job hunt."

Jeffrey was close to tears. This is not how it was supposed to end for him. The blood wouldn't leave his hands now.

"Please, sir! I've done everything you asked. You said this was a good offering for the Chairman. I'll even scrub toilets. Please."

Bronson sighed.

The foreign whispering voice echoed again through the room.

"It seems our generous Chairman has a soft spot for you."

Jeffrey teared-up with gratitude.

"He wishes to meet with you in person"

Mr. Stanley and Mr. Graf grabbed Jeffrey by the arms and stood him up, holding him steady.

Mr. Bronson spoke an unrecognizable language, then whistled.

The conference table split in two and separated, revealing a massive pit spitting flames and gas. A choir of cries shrieked in agony and pleas for mercy.

The partners dragged Jeffrey towards the pit. He resisted as best he could.

As he struggled to break free, Jeffrey cried, "What are you doing?"

"Making the proper introductions to our Chairman."

The partners cried out in unison, "Hail, Mammon! Hail the Prince of Riches!" And they threw Jeffrey into the pit and watched the flames embrace him.

The conference table rejoined and the partners took their seats.

Mr. Stanley said, "If that doesn't satisfy our Lord, I don't know what will."

"Agreed," said Mr. Graf. "I do enjoy a good show, but six sacrifices is far too much. What does this mean?"

Mr. Bronson gulped down his bourbon. "It means, gentlemen, that we must continue to make our head count until we've reached the satisfactory quota. Our Lord has always taken care of us. Every recession, depression, and correction, he has delivered for us. Until we reach the quote, it's business as usual."

The conference phone buzzed, and Mr. Graf hit the speaker button. A young voice squeaked, "I have Ms. Victoria Carrol in the lobby for you sir. Her second interview."

Mr. Stanley and Mr. Graf snickered and cackled.

Mr. Bronson walked over to the bar to refill his glass. He took a slow sip and smiled. "Send her up"

Feast

I an Jackson was a staunch professional.

At 5 a.m., Monday through Friday, he'd leap out of bed to catch the downtown bus to Providence for the breakfast buffet at Chimi's Kitchen.

Ten dollars a plate was the agreed upon price. He'd race around the hot and cold trays, pushing away any sorry peasant who was too slow to simply grab and go.

In a flash, Ian scooped up sausage patties, pancakes slathered with butter and syrup, hash browns, scrambled eggs that were seasoned just right, strips of turkey bacon, more sausages, and a tall glass of orange juice to wash everything down.

He skipped the fruit cups. Not worth it in his humble opinion.

Ian squeezed into his custom corner booth, built to compensate for his weight of three hundred and sixty two pounds, and sucked down everything on his plate, not leaving even the tiniest crumb. He stacked the empty plate at the center of the table and went back to the trays of food.

By the end of breakfast, Ian received fifty bucks in his checking account. Before, all you needed was a picture of your finished plates sent to your bank to confirm, but other Eaters had taken advantage of the old system.

Now, the Brand Corporation required all Eaters to have small monitors attached to the lining of their stomachs to track food intake as well as digestion.

Ian liked to walk to the Great Woods Dragon down the street for the Chinese buffet next. Sure, it was smaller compared to the others, but he needed to ease his stomach. The pork fried rice, though it smelled divine that afternoon, often left his gut feeling greasy and rough for the rest of the day.

Grace, the owner, had Ian's booth ready for him, with his bib and moist hand towelettes. He descended upon the lunch buffet with nothing held back.

Skipping the rice, he attacked and devoured the crispy chicken fingers drowned in duck sauce, the pad tai mixed with peanut sauce, and boneless spare ribs just as quickly as he had gobbled up his breakfast.

He licked his fingers at the sound of the push notification from his phone: eighty dollars deposited.

After letting his stomach rest for thirty minutes, he made a trek down the road for an early dinner at Ron's Ribs & BBQ. Afternoons were harder and it was difficult for him to keep up, but the money was too good to pass.

Providence was hardly a city anymore. Long gone were the college town, the beautiful campuses, and the vibrant spirit of its people. The city was bathed in shadowy smog, gloomed by towering corporate high rises. Many of the city folk set up camps in the old parks, even squatting in abandoned shops. The city was coated in night everlasting.

When Ian made it to the BBQ joint, he was startled by an older man in tattered clothes, sitting on the stoop of the restaurant door.

"I need to get by," Ian said, covering his nose with his sauce-drenched sleeve.

The man looked to be in his forties, his beard tinted in a nasty amber, his hair slippery and hanging over his dirty face. He didn't budge.

"I said I need to get by," Ian said again.

The man growled. "Fuck off, fatty. This is my spot. Go find your own!"

"You're blocking my way."

The man looked at Ian hard and began to chuckle softly.

"Something funny?" Ian asked.

"You're all the same. You fucking fatties all over the place."

"Excuse me?"

"You think just because someone pays you to pig out that gives you thee right to treat people like shit and bark orders?"

Ian ignored the homeless man, turned, and continued down the road.

The man followed him. "You think 'cause you're the one of the few left with a job that makes you special? Huh?"

Ian hustled a little faster.

"Go ahead! Go eat yourself to death, you dumb son of a bitch. Go and stuff your face for easy cash."

Ian started to run as best he could, but he couldn't escape the heckles. The words were banging away in his ear.

"You'll never be free like me! You hear me, you fat fuck? You'll never. Be. Free!"

Ian turned the corner of the block and fell over a heap of trash. He was huffing and grabbing at his chest. Little beams of sweat trickled down his face. His cheeks were hot and crimson. His vision became blurry and then turned black.

***

There was a slow, steady succession of beeps as Ian opened his eyes to bright lights. There were tubes in his nose, and he was wrapped in a baby-blue Johnny gown. And IV dangled above his head. The bitter smell of industrial cleaner was enough to keep his head spinning.

A tall, fit, well-groomed man dressed in black scrubs and a face mask entered the room. The young doctor smiled. "How are we, Mr. Jackson?"

"What happened?" Ian asked, his strength diminished.

"I'm Dr. Walton. You're in a Brand Corp Treatment Facility just outside of downtown. There was a slight hiccup with your stomach monitor. But everything is taken care of."

Ian struggled to keep his eyes open and follow what the young doctor was telling him.

"Hiccup? What—what does that mean?"

"A small hiccup, yes. Usually caused by a sudden spike in stress levels. I checked your records when you were brought in this evening. Your stats are excellent. Perfectly healthy. I see you're a hard earner also."

"Really?"

"Why, yes. You have an excellent track record. The Health Board Director has never been so impressed. You are a model patient it seems."

Ian smiled and let out a sigh of relief. All seven members of the City Health Board had signed off on the Brand Corporation's Eater Program, something to help revitalize the stagnant economy.

"So I can go home? Right?"

Dr. Watson turned to the health chart and read Ian's stats. He didn't say anything.

"Doctor?"

"Yes," Dr. Watson said, but he kept his eyes on the digital charts. "I think you'll be able to go home." He paused. "However—" For a moment, he said nothing.

The doctor's pause sent a small shiver through Ian's body. He watched the doctor swipe through the digital records, strong green eyes moving side to side in tune with the cold beeps of the machines connected to Ian.

"I would still like to run a few more tests. Just to be certain everything is...in order."

"Is that really necessary? You said I was—"

"You are, Mr. Jackson, you are. A model patient for sure. But we at the center prefer to be safe rather than sorry. The health of our patients is our highest concern."

Ian continued listening to the beeps of his heart monitor. By God, a model patient? Ian had never been considered a model for anything in his life. His father had ignored him, and he found his mother overbearing.

Like a proper schoolmistress, she kept him on a strict daily schedule regarding chores, hygiene, and diet. He had endured beatings when he wasn't fast enough to complete one of her tasks, and he had gone many nights without food. It brought her tremendous joy to starve her darling boy.

"Keep the fat off, Ian darling," she had often said.

Her condescending tone haunted him. When her death finally came, he had shed no tears, and his stomach rejoiced.

***

The Brand Corp built a testing facility for Eaters and monitored them overnight. The intimate dining hall was supplied with enough food to feed a battalion of hungry soldiers.

Hanging high above the dining hall were the Observatory Suites, occupied by an eager Dr. Watson and a couple of overworked, underpaid lab assistants observing, studying, and documenting.

Dr. Watson led the Observation Team that afternoon and took great care in recording everything his eye could capture. The team monitored closely for certain details: each morsel of food consumed; any and all accouterments; flavorings, sweeteners, and seasonings that were added or avoided; the pace of chewing; how the stomach responded to certain foods; and other concerns sent in by the Health Board.

Ian was given a facility scooter for easier mobility. He scooted his way to the jumbo shrimp and cocktail sauce, then downed a few mini-donuts, and gobbled up the deli meats of turkey, low-sodium ham, and roast beef.

***

Ian sat alone in his little scooter stuffing his mouth with a ham sandwich. The honey dijon mustard dripped all over his Johhny gown. The overnight tests had seemed easy. He debated whether he should ask for some compensation arrangement to make up for lost time.

He glanced down at his scooter as a red stress ball rolled up and hit his tire. He looked up, and in came a little boy. He was about seven and dressed in a little baby-blue suit.

Ian smiled. He hadn't seen a young child in years. Especially not a clean, healthy one.

The little boy walked closer to Ian and picked up the ball.

Ian smiled again, but the boy just looked at Ian with one part in fascination, the other part bewilderment.

"Hello, little one."

The boy didn't say anything. He continued staring.

"My name is Ian. What's yours?"

The boy looked away.

"That's okay. I just—I don't see many kids around these days. Are you from the city? Where are your parents?"

The boy squeezed the stress ball in his fist repeatedly.

In a refined and wise tone, the little boy said, "You are quite large."

Ian sighed. He placed his sandwich in the basket of his scooter and wiped his mouth, then asked, "Would you like to play catch?" Ian asked

The boy froze with bewilderment, but then smiled and nodded. He stepped back and they tossed the little stress ball back and forth to the boy's delight.

"You still didn't tell me your name."

"I don't have one."

Ian caught the ball and held it for a moment. "What do you mean you don't have one? Everyone has a name."

"I can assure you, I don't have a name. Father has always referred to me as 'boy'."

Ian tossed the ball again, "Gee that's—that's sad. What do the other kids call you?"

"Father says I'm not allowed to play with the other children in the facility. He says they are not children, but lost animals."

"I don't understand. What other children are—"

"Father!"

Dr. Samuel P. Burke, the Director of the Health Board, entered the dining room. He stood straight and had a regal air about him. He was tucked and neatly packaged in his white lab coat, and his face was clean of any imperfections.

"Why are you out here? Return to your room, boy! You will wait until the ceremony."

The boy dropped his ball and scurried away.

"Mr. Jackson. At last." The director's eyes were dark, brooding, and tired. Eyes that could tell you stories of every patient who came through his facility.

"I am Dr. Burke, Director of the Health Board and Chair of the Medical Unit at the Brand Corporation. I've been looking forward to meeting you, young man. I am most impressed by your—record."

"Really?"

"Oh, yes of course. The Health Board is looking to expand the Eater Program. The Board is hosting a small ceremony for the national medical community to demonstrate our miraculous results."

"Miraculous?"

"Why yes, of course. Your efforts in the Program will save thousands of lives, Ian. The Brand Corporation has agreed to increase our funding in order for us to continue our work to do good. The Program is just the beginning."

Ian's heart began to race. He felt the director's passion for his work, and understood the man's tired eyes.

"Will you help us, Ian?"

A rising sound of voices echoed from outside the dining hall. Then the door kicked out and in came a woman, mid-thirties, with ragged hair and clothing and a beaten face. She was screaming.

Dr. Watson tried to hold her off.

"You!" cried the nervous woman "Take it! Take it all back!" In a fit, she hurled a paper bag at the director and struggled to remain standing.

Rolls of cash slipped from the bag as it hit the floor.

The woman shrieked, "My babies! Where are my babies?"

Dr. Watson looked at Ian. "I apologize, sir. I've called Security. They will be here soon."

The woman spat at the director's shoes and lunged for Ian.

Dr. Watson lunged just as quickly at the woman to pull her off of him.

"Take the bag back! I want my babies! Give me back my babies!"

Dr. Watson looked up just as four men from the security team rushed into the room. "Remove this woman!"

The men dragged the screaming, ragged woman out of the room.

Dr. Watson composed himself and turned back to Ian. "Nothing to worry about, Mr. Jackson. A former patient of ours. I'm sure you're aware of the rampant drug problem in the city."

"Yes," Ian said with a sigh. "So many poor children."

"Yes," Watson said. "Born to parents fighting addiction. Fortunately, we have plans to help address the growing crisis."

Ian frowned. "How can I help?"

Dr. Watson smiled.

***

The following morning, Ian agreed to attend the ceremony hosted by Dr. Burke and his medical staff. He expressed concern that he didn't have the proper attire for a formal function. Not anything that would fit at least. But the doctor said a simple Johnny was all that was expected.

Ian was helped into a wheelchair and wheeled to the platform next to the stage of the Great Auditorium. A sea of white lab coats flooded the hall.

The country's top medical professionals awaited the special announcement prepared by the good doctor.

Ian's hands trembled. He was not fond of crowds, but it was all for a good cause. On the stage, the little boy in the blue suit was standing next to the great podium.

Ian waved and smiled at him.

The boy smiled back.

As the murmuring and chatter died, Dr. Burke took the stage. He stood behind the podium, regal as ever, and pulled a small scrap of paper from the side pocket of his coat.

Slowly, he said, "I prepared these words over a month ago."

As he began to read his words, he paused and sighed. He looked up at his medical colleagues.

Some of them were holding hands. A few others were fighting back tears.

Dr. Burke smiled. "So much has changed in the past month. Glorious change." He gestured with the paper. "These words bear little meaning now, I suppose."

His voice carried great authority, passion, and neat precision as it echoed throughout the hall. He scrapped the paper, tossed it aside, and began again with fresh optimism for the glory he was about to announce.

"Twelve years ago, the Brand Corporation and the city of Providence looked to us, the finest medical minds in the nation, to combat two glaring issues sweeping the country."

The hall fell silent, the audience leaning in to hear the good word like faithful parishioners.

Even Ian was enraptured by the words of the doctor.

"Growing hunger among adults and children and unprecedented unemployment levels have gripped modern society by the throat. Through years of research, government red tape, medical setbacks, and other unforeseen obstacles, I am proud to declare Phase One has exceeded all expectations. The Eater Program has reduced joblessness to pre-epidemic levels in just one year."

The audience rose to their feet amid roaring cheers and loud applause.

Dr. Burke extended his hands, palms down. "Settle down, now. The best is yet to come!" He turned his attention to Ian Jackson and smiled.,

Ian couldn't help but smile back. For the first time in years, he felt useful. He looked out at the crowd as the cheering died down and smiled again. He felt seen. He felt worthy. He felt—special.

The doctor looked at the audience again. "Ladies and gentlemen, before I continue on with Phase Two, I'd like to acknowledge the man who is about to make history. Glorious history."

The doctor extended his hand out to his side as the lights of the hall dimmed and the spotlight settled upon Ian.

"Mr. Ian Jackson, a Providence native and a hard-working man, has become a rising star of the Eater Program, He is Brand Corp's highest earner, and living proof of the success of our efforts."

The crowd roared once more like Super Bowl spectators.

Ian had started to perspire under the bright light, but he was grateful no one could see the teardrops running down his face.

"Ian's charity does not end there," Dr. Burke said "He has graciously accepted his role in helping our team tackle Phase Two. For years, junkheads in this city have sold their children for drugs and other favors. These poor lots have been neglected, born with severe medical defects, and they continue to go hungry." He paused and gestured toward Ian again. "But not anymore. Thanks to Mr. Jackson's work today, we can begin to eradicate child hunger."

He paused again and turned to Ian. "Mr. Jackson, your sacrifice today shall not be forgotten."

Ian stopped smiling.

The platform below his wheelchair shook. And before he realized what was happening, a trapdoor below him split open. He screamed as he fell through and slammed into the dirt. On both sides and behind him were concrete walls. Each wall had a camera mounted on it.

Dr. Burke raised his right hand. "Release the children!"

Below the auditorium in the dusty darkness, Ian heard cages rattling. Then the doors of the cages swung open, and several beastly creatures, marred in soot, bony and scarred, were released. They howled and barked, scratching at the dirt.

One creature stopped, its nose testing the air to catch a sharp, ripe whiff. It slowly looked around and locked eyes with Ian.

The others followed, crawling towards the terrified prey.

Dr. Burke raised a tiny, silver bell above his head. As he gave it a jingle, he whispered into the microphone. "Children," he said. "It's dinner time."

The young creatures rushed to Ian, trampling each other, fighting and clawing their way to their meal.

Ian, with all his remaining strength, picked himself up and clawed at a concrete wall, looking for any escape.

His fingernails were peeled back and bleeding, and the skin of his chubby fingers was ripped and raw.

His screaming was drowned-out by the heckles and shouts of the rowdy, captivated audience.

Ian looked back, his face white and his eyes wide, and watched as over a dozen beastly beings charged at him with unrelenting speed. A warm sensation ran down his thick left leg. He looked down. He had wet himself.

The savage little beasts howled and screeched as Ian stood helpless, frozen in his own piss.

Within seconds, his body was ripped apart by ravenous little claws. Little teeth pierced and sank into his flesh. His bones cracked, and his tissue was ripped apart.

Ian was still alive. As the children dined, he screamed, "Help!" and "Please!" and "Oh God!"

The hall erupted in cackling cheers at the sight and sound of the horror.

The little boy in blue stood alone next to Dr. Burke, watching as the display monitor captured the event. He clapped his hands over his eyes. "Father, I do not wish to watch this."

"*Look* at it, boy! This is my life's work. If you are to succeed me, you'll need a stronger stomach."

The little boy peeked through his fingers and watched the monitor. He looked at the remnants of the man known to him as Ian Jackson, professional Eater and test subject number 941. The boy could still hear Ian's cries.

The boy looked up at his father. "The man keeps yelling the word, 'God'. What is that, father?"

Dr. Burke brushed the boy away, "Never mind that, my child. You are witnessing something far more important."

"What is that?"

Dr. Burke smiled, "Progress, my boy. Progress."

The boy turned back to the grotesque display.

Finally, Burke took the child by the hand and led him away. "Come now. Let the children feast."

Illuminatus For a Penny-a-Word

The industrial coffee maker groaned as it released the fresh brew into his stained mug.

Pete Graf watched the blackness fill to the brim. The hints of sweet, rich chocolate sent him back to his youth when his mother would surprise him with a 5th Avenue chocolate bar for his birthday. But that was so long ago. He'd give anything for a good old-fashioned chocolate bar now. He meant *old* fashioned, not one that was artificially made in some cold factory wrapped together with the arms of a machine.

He stretched his back, careful not to bust up the spinal-chip implant that was nestled between his skull and his cervical vertebrae. For 145 years Pete's routine was the same. He always arrived two hours before his shift started at 9 am. His uniform was a pair of khakis held up by dark-brown suspenders and a clean white short-sleeve shirt with a purple tie. Always a purple tie. Not lavender. Not magenta. Plain purple.

Each white shirt would be neatly pressed every morning at 5 a.m. without fail. After each shift, he'd polish his shoes until they were gleaming. He never took his thirty-minute lunch as advised. From 8 a.m. until 6 p.m., he sat at his Olympia SM4 manual typewriter, the latest model he was afforded, and punched the keys in his small closet of an office. On nights when his boss asked for a last-minute revision, Pete parked his butt in his small, wooden chair and cranked out another 4,000 words. Some nights the tips of his fingers would be wrapped in bandages to stop the bleeding.

Pete did what he was told. He was a good company man.

He had spent much of his adult life sweating over a typewriter like a workhorse from his early days of submitting stories to science fiction and weird horror pulp magazines. That's how he had made his bread during the height of the Great Depression.

Cold nights alone hammering keys occupied his time when he wasn't busy sucking down a bottle of gin or scraping together crackers and soup at the local diner. Sleeping in motels, hiding his car all over 5th Avenue from repo men, and wearing the same beaten-up slacks and loafers was not a life he missed.

A man in the black pinstripe suit had approached him with an offer: free room and board, three hot meals a day, and the opportunity to do a great service to his country during the war effort.

Pete had jumped for joy and accepted halfway through the man's pitch. He was no soldier though. He wouldn't carry an M1 carbine anywhere in Europe or Japan. His asthma had put a stop to that possibility. This was a different type of service.

In order to move forward with the job, Pete had needed a quick procedure done. A surgeon made small incision at the top of his vertebrae for the placement of a microchip. It would freeze the aging process and keep his body fit and as healthy as a young man perpetually 30 years old. It sounded like something from one of his science fiction yarns, but a steady income was hard to pass up.

He signed on the dotted line and became a staff writer for the United States Government, penning political conspiracies, prolonging the war with Hitler's army a few more decades, and keeping the nation in perpetual fear. All this could be done in his basement office far from the eyes of the public.

American scientists had developed a breakthrough; something that would turn the tide of the war in favor of the Allies without the use of nuclear arms. In lieu of killing Nazis on the front lines with rifles and tanks, Pete would use his skills as a pulp writer to craft clever stories on his manual Olympia SM4 typewriter. He could bend reality through the written word.

The Invasion of Sicily deployed 500 Rocket Men instead of thousands of Allied troops to topple Mussolini's regime in half a day. Pete's use of big, silver flying saucers raining hellfire blasts from above on the beach of Normandy drove Nazi forces in full retreat.

As it turned out, his trusty SM4 proved more powerful than the bomb.

Pete went back to his desk and took his seat in front of his typewriter. He put a clean, white piece of paper behind the platen and rolled it through just right. Then he cracked his knuckles and was ready for a day's work. Just before he began to type, he reached for his coffee mug and brought it to his lips for a slow sip.

He spat it right back out. Brown droplets rained down on his clean paper.

He wished his tongue was burned off from the scorching steam of his coffee rather than taste the chalky bitterness that filled his cup. Shit.

"They changed the coffee," he muttered. "A century on the job, day-in and day-out and they changed the coffee?"

A low growl from behind Pete's desk said, "Shush it, Petey! I can't concentrate with you yapping."

Behind Pete sat Freddy Rockwell, a short, well fed, chain-smoking, grizzly man in his fifties. Freddy was Pete's only co-worker in the whole department.

Freddy kept typing away with ferocious passion, keeping his typewriter red hot. "You're drinking too much of that cheap crap anyway. Your body is telling you to quit."

Pete sank into his chair and slipped the mug away from him. "Have you tried it, Freddy? It's off. The whole thing is off."

"Tastes the same to me. I'll stick with my regular duo of Johnny and Jack, thank you!"

Pete scratched his head and took another sip. Gentle this time. He needed to be sure. A few swirls were enough to render the verdict. He hawked his mouthful of dirty, hot water back into the mug.

"I don't get it. It smells the same and everything. But it's...different. Why would they change it?"

"Quit yapping and get typing," Freddy said. "We're getting a new assignment, remember?"

Pete sighed softly and slid the mug as far away from him as he could. He found the white envelope on his right side with his name and today's date printed in red ink. He ripped it open. When he unfolded the white paper, his assignment was revealed in a sentence: Economic Hardshop on the Rise! Mega Corporation to Unveil New Corpo-States to Curtail Homelessness!

In a flash and without a moment's hesitation, Pete's fingers were pounding away at the SM4's keys. At 149 words a minute, he could quickly hammer out a story based on the title alone, even with only two fingers punching the keys.

Pete never knew the origin of the SM4 or its power to fabricate new realities at will. He never thought to ask. Besides, it was not his business to know these things. Every morning a freshly sealed envelope would show up at his desk like clockwork. He'd rip it open, read the sentence, and get busy typing. That was it.

His only instruction from the man who had hired him was to write a new story based on the sentence in the envelope. Within minutes, the story he'd penned would be brought to life. From his typewriter to the evening news, the story would become reality no matter how ridiculous or absurd. If it was printed in the paper, it would all come true.

Pete and Freddy had known each other in their old life, but only in passing. They were too busy submitting to magazine editors and churning out stories to give each other so much as a "hello." Since they first signed on to this job, the fictioneers managed not to kill each other in their cramped, pathetic basement office.

The sharp, snapping click and clack of punched keys filled the room followed by the occasional bell that rang just before the slam of the carriage.

Freddy slammed his SM4 lever hard to the left, mumbling the words he'd just written on the page to himself. "Dammit," he said. "The keys keep sticking. Every time."

"You hit the keys too hard. Be nicer to your machine and it'll treat you better."

Freddy rolled his eyes. "And the platen on this thing needs replacing. The whole damn thing's a mess."

Pete ignored him and kept typing.

Freddy said, "The Department of Defense practically gets a blank check in the name of patriotism, and we get stuck with these faulty desktops. We won the last war with our own two fingers, but we're stuck living in a cellar hole. Why did they give us Olympias and not one of those supercomputers everyone's using now?"

Freddy was hot.

"I mean, I can learn. And we *gotta* ask for a bump in pay, Petey. This 10 cents-a-word crap ain't cutting it. I gotta cover my expenses."

Pete's eyes lit up. "Expenses? What expenses? We got meals covered, at night we sleep on a cot, and we got over 5,000 channels on the tube to turn our brains into mush. What expenses can you possibly have?"

Freddy let out a big sigh of frustration. "Sometimes I like to upscale my dining experience and order from the upstairs kitchen."

Pete looked confused, "But they give us food free here!"

"You call a bowl of porridge, tasteless crackers, and a fruit cup food? If I'm gonna work for these G-men I want the best food money can buy. So I negotiated an expense account with the upstairs kitchen. The cost's a bit steep, but the food is better."

"Negotiate for better coffee then, ya chowhound."

Freddy reached under his desk and pulled out a half-empty bottle of Jack Daniels and kicked his feet up. "I think I'll take a half-day today. Not many exciting things are happening."

Pete was silent. He ran his finger over the last few sentences before ripping the paper out of the machine and tearing it to pieces.

"You work too hard, Petey. Here, have a drink. Relax," Freddy poured a helping of whiskey into a shot glass until it almost overflowed.

Pete rubbed his temples, ignoring Fred's offer. "Maybe I'll write a letter to the boss. Maybe we can get better coffee by Christmas?"

Fred downed a shot. "Petey, enough with the damn coffee."

"I just don't understand. The whole pot is off."

"Things change, my friend. You can't get too comfortable."

"We've been at this for over 100 years, Fred. Why change things now?"

"Who the hell cares? We carry out orders from the bosses upstairs. End of story. To the world, we don't even exist. Enjoy the ride, Pete."

They heard the rattling of the elevator cage descending. They both knew it was only used by one person: the man who had hired them all those years ago.

Pete wiped his shiny forehead with his arm and loosened his tie a bit. The boss never came down to their office in the catacombs except on special conditions like an urgent assignment. One that could not be marked by a government paper trail. One that had to be kept off the books.

Pete fumbled through his pockets, looking for a cigarette to take the edge off. "The boss man? Here? Whatcha think he's got this time?"

"No idea," Freddy said. "Maybe he needs us to whack another president like that last one who kept poking his nose all over the place? Kenneston? I think that was his name."

"No, this feels different. I don't like it."

The elevator bell dinged as the doors parted. A man in a three-piece, black-pinstripe suit emerged from the dimly lit cage. He was tall with slicked-back hair and sharp-looking glasses. A well-put-together presentation.

"Fancy seeing you down here." Freddy grinned. "It ain't often the president's errand boy makes a house call these days."

The lips of the man in black stretched into a fake grin as he pulled a thin, golden case from his jacket pocket. He was Edgar Clarke, the chief of staff to the president of the United States. Unofficially, he also oversaw Pete and Freddy's entire department.

He said, "Well, gentlemen, it looks like this is where we part ways." He opened his case, took out a thin, white cigarette, and brought it to his lips. "In a few hours, the boys from upstairs will come down and clear out the place."

As Clarke pulled out his matchbox , Pete's jaw practically hit the floor.

"We're *fired*?" Fred slammed his pudgy hands on the desk. "How do ya like that? Just when I was getting used to over a century of servitude."

Pete said, "B-but Mr. Clarke, I don't understand. Are you *replacing* us? Was there a problem with the copy on the last assignment?"

Clarke took a long puff and blew it into the room. "Boys, you've been a great asset to this nation and have handled your roles beautifully. But I'm afraid the president has new initiatives he wants to achieve the old-fashioned way." He flipped an ash off his cigarette. "Besides, with the economy tanking and inflation in the double digits, the government has decided to liquidate some of its assets and sell off certain departments to some corporate buyers."

"How do ya like that?" Freddy chuckled. "I didn't even know the government *could* sell off departments. I learn something dumb every day."

Pete sank into his chair and laid his face in his hands. Decades of service to a company that provided the simple comfort of hot meals, housing, and decent pay, and it was all about to be taken away from him. He finally found that lone cigarette lingering in his pocket, but instead he wished he had that shitty cup of coffee from earlier. That certainly would have knocked the dumbfounded expression off his face.

He looked at Mr. Clarke. "Sir, what's gonna happen to me and Freddy? The world out there and—it's different. Ol' Fred and I haven't been back to New York since Superman debuted in Action Comics." He paused. "I read the papers, Mr. Clarke, and I watch the news reporters on the set in my room before bed each night. They got cars that drive themselves now. Everyone's glued to the little blue screens they hold in front of their faces. And guys like Freddy and me—they—we just don't exist anymore. Not in this world anyway."

Clarke's eyes were fixed on Pete. His duty as chief of staff was simply to keep the writers in line and have each order carried out with no questions asked. Nannying was not part of his job description, and boredom quickly soured his mood.

He hesitated for a moment and took a long puff, filling his lungs with cheap smoke as Pete's question lingered in the air. "Well, I may have something. One of the MegaCorps is looking to expand its entertainment business to something called "immersed reality television." As luck would have it, they're looking for a writer to staff."

"Look at that," said Fred. "We're movin' on up, Petey. First government work, now writing for TV. I'd prefer old-school radio, but beggars can't be choosers."

Pete said, "How much are they offering?"

Clarke smiled as a cloud of smoke passed through his lips. "MegaCorp is offering twenty cents a word."

Pete froze with his eyes wide open.

Freddy whispered, "Twenty?"

"Oh," Mr. Clarke turned toward the elevator, "I'm not sure if I mentioned this before, but they only need one writer for the job."

Freddy and Pete quickly glanced at one another.

Fred muttered, "What would happen to the guy who doesn't get the job?"

Mr. Clarke looked back., "Decommissioned. Along with the rest of the department."

Fred's face turned read as he came to a boil. "Now hold on!"

Pete shook his head. "Decommissioned? Just like that? After all we've done for you?"

"I don't write the rules, boys. We're the executive branch." Mr. Clarke pulled a white envelope from the breast pocket and tore it open.

"Here's the contract. Who'll be the first to sign?"

Freddy scrambled for a fresh sheet of white paper to jam into the SM4 with a panic, hoping to write his boss out of existence with the power of the typewriter. The back of his neck lit up with a crisp, clear blue spark.

He jerked out of the chair, falling on the floor as his body tightened.

Pete rushed over to Freddy. Mr. Clarke's thumb was pinned to a red button on a handheld buzzer.

Pete glared at him. "What have you done?" Then he looked at his colleague again. Fred!" He

knelt over his partner and held his head steady in spite of his seizure.

Mr. Clarke eased his thumb off the buzzer.

"Looks like it's just you, Mr. Graf. Unless, of course, you wish to be scrapped as well like Mr. Rockwell."

Pete watched as Freddy's eyes turned blood-red and his body ceased to shake. His colleague had been written out with the click of a button. A sudden chill gripped the back of his neck. Was any of this worth it? Decade after decade of taking orders from government handlers in exchange for living in subpar conditions, and what did he or Freddy have to show for it? He could take the new job, sure, but this was not the life he had imagined for himself. He wrote shlock after all, and he barely got by on his own.

Mr. Clarke gently caressed the red button. "Well?"

Pete stood up and turned towards his employer. "Where do I sign?"

Mr. Clarke smiled and held out his fountain pen.

Pete did what he was told. He was a good company man.

Quota

The smoke from his stamped-out cigarette still danced in the air high above him. His eye occupied the rifle scope even after he had watched the target drop to the asphalt moments ago.

Tim exhaled and raised his head slowly. The hard earth supported his body and the gentle wind brushed against his face as he watched the evening sun retreat for the day. He enjoyed the view from up here; the moment's stillness and beautiful, majestic orange ball sent his mind into a meditative state of ease.

But these were not peaceful times.

He rarely had the opportunity to come up and visit the Surface Level unless his work demanded it. The Surface Level was a metropolitan graveyard of skyscrapers long abandoned by Corporate America and the real estate moguls.

Being a Head Hunter was no easy task these days.

When the Third World War concluded and the Upper Levels were blasted into dust, the factory owners retreated down below, resuming operations deep in the catacombs. The Corporate Barons needed bodies to operate their factories, and survivors like Tim needed work. He shook hands with the Devil and became a Hunter, scouring the wastelands above for bodies, and dragging doped-up junkheads down to the auction block to be sold to the highest bidder.

Helluva way to make a living.

He received the alert on his comms: Fifty Minutes Until Market Close.

He stood up, wiped the dirt and pebbles from his chest and legs, then fished his binoculars out of his backpack and scanned the view before him.

A message appeared in the binoculars. Target identified: Alive.

He gathered his equipment, made his way to his Hypersport motorbike, and mounted. The Hypersport emitted a low growl and hiss, then the engine clearing its throat with a metallic purr. Rumbling and waiting. He donned a black camo helmet, complementing his rough garb. He rolled the throttle and the motorbike roared as he dashed toward the open road heading for his target.

Tim zoomed through empty streets. Everywhere there were burned-out condominiums, trash heaps, and boarded-up shops and outlets where the tired owners barely clung to their hope of a better future. Where people lived on the scraps left behind by the manufacturing plants and sold at auction by their foreign overlords. The tech giants that sucked up whatever remaining spirit the working classes had left.

Junkheads, homeless squatters, and hungry dogs made up the Surface Level Prescient. For guys like Tim, everyone was fair game.

He pulled up a few feet from his target. He dismounted, armed with a blaster set for stun.

The target was there, lying on his side. His breathing was shallow, his chest barely rising up and down.

Tim's heartbeat kicked up as he carefully approached him from behind. He gripped the blaster and aimed at the body.

He followed the trail of blood on the asphalt. The night had arrived and the street lamps had flicked on. A beam of light shimmered over the dark body. The target was long, lean, and wearing nothing but gym shorts and a graphic tee, lying on the hard ground, shaking and bleeding from the bullet wound in his leg.

He looked at Tim and mumbled a word or two.

Tim pulled out his worn-out notebook and read the description: black male, late 20s, slender build. He thumbed to another page and continued reading. Experience: none required.

The young man on the cold ground started to speak again.

Tim locked eyes with him.

The young man's face was reflected on Tim's helmet. "Please," he whispered. "Kill me."

The comms alerted him: Thirty Minutes Until Market Close.

Tim holstered his blaster and placed the cybernetic handcuffs on his target. He lifted the man and strapped him tightly into the sidecar of the motorbike. Another roar of the engine and they disappeared into the night.

***

The iron cage rattled as it descended below the earth, returning to the UnderCity, the industrial hellscape where Tim earned his living. He turned to his target, who was still shivering, most likely due to his last hit than the fear of being sold at the auction.

The cage elevator stopped with a shudder at the ground floor.

Tim grabbed his prize by the throat as the doors creaked open and dragged him out. He hustled through the crowded street of the busy plaza, hundreds of wealthy buyers and patrons eyeing rare gemstone jewelry, recycled artwork that decorated the walls, and precious strips of dog meat hanging from stall hooks.

The young man's face was petrified. He had wet himself in fright, probably an effect of the Juju powder he'd likely taken.

They approached the towering steel gate. The Welcome Shack stood just outside it below flashing neon-colored lights, barely held together after years of use. Inside the Welcome Shack, Tim rang the chrome desk bell as he pushed the young man to his knees.

A great, burly figure shuffled from the shadows and appeared at the front desk. He was bear-like and gruff. He spoke with a slow timbre and a thick Eastern accent. "I feared you would not make it in time."

"Barely," Tim said. "Got time to clean this one up for the auction, Stepan?"

Stepan the Cleaner, who lived in the shack, reached over the desk with his large, rough hands and examined the face of the target, going over every detail. He ran his fingers through the man's mouth twice. "I should reject your catch for such a late arrival."

"C'mon, Step! It's been a shit month. Help me out."

Stepan groaned a low growl. He scratched his forehead and said, "For you, my friend, I do this. But for double credit price."

"Double?"

Stepan nodded. "Mmhm."

"You know how to kick a guy when he's down, you greedy bastard."

Stepan emitted a smoky cackle. "Difficult times good for business. I make more when Head Hunters under pressure."

"So it seems." Tim threw a pouch of silver coins onto the desk. "He's all yours."

Stepan rolled his rough hand over a large lever and slammed it down. The front gates slowly shifted open and Tim made his way inside alone. As the gates closed, the sign hanging high above turned a neon pink reading: AUCTION.

A feminine voice rang out through the busy plaza reminding bidders that all sales would be final.

The plaza was grand and opulent, fit for a rich sultan of the east. Merchants from the wastelands far away flooded to the auction to sell their goods in hopes of securing sponsorship contracts from the Corporate Barons.

In the center of the inner plaza was a stage. Over a dozen men and women were dressed in tattered clothes and held together in cybernetic handcuffs. The races, colors, ages and heights and weights varied: black, brown, tan, pink, white, and yellow, young, middle-aged, and old, tall and short, fat and thin.

As the crowd began to gather, Tim fished for a cigarette and disappeared quietly among the sea of spectators, blending into the shadows.

It was all routine. Freshly poached stock would stand on the stage and be sold to the highest bidder. It was unusual for a Head Hunter to watch a live auction. Most of them dumped the bodies at the Cleaner and waited with a hard drink at the local tavern. Under normal circumstances, Tim would have joined them.

His eyes narrowed as he searched the stage. The last arrival, his catch from the evening, all cuffed, cleaned, and bandaged around one leg, made it.

No time to relax just yet. Only the easy part was over.

He watched as the Corporate Barons shuffled high above in their plush box seats. Then the Auctioneer took the stage and hushed the crowd.

Tim stood in the distance, watching, smoking, and quietly praying to any higher power that would take his call that evening. Please sell.

The alarm came and the bidding wars began.

The Barons each reviewed the stock on the auction block.

Bidding paddles came up and down swiftly.

Silver coins exchanged hands.

One by one, the stock was dragged off the stage and thrown into dingy shuttle buses.

Tim flicked ash off his cigarette. His catch was up next.

The Auctioneer did his job, highlighting the stock's physical features, background, and ethnicity. He was a real showman earning his pay.

Tim took another drag. Please sell.

The Barons, perched above in their nest of wealth and power, said nothing at first. The fat cats puffed on overpriced cigars, sipped Spanish wine, and seemed aloof or disinterested.

Tim whispered, "C'mon, you bastards~" He anxiously took another drag.

He watched their round, old faces stiffen as if they were displeased. Then each of them slowly rose to their feet and disappeared from sight.

The cigarette dropped out of Tim's mouth. The Auctioneer was silent, the young stock was shoved off stage, and the final bell chimed, announcing the auction was concluded.

***

Slouched over the bar counter, Tim let out a sigh before chugging down his pint of beer. He quickly ordered a second.

In the dimly lit tavern, he sat alone with his shame, bad luck, and a tall empty glass.

He rubbed his left temple, wondering what was next for him now that he had officially missed quota.

Another pint made its way to Tim's hand. He fixated on the liquid amber and took a slow sip. He might as well enjoy himself. Not much time left.

"Next one's on me." A small pouch of silver coins dropped on the counter. "You look like you're gonna need it." The voice was deep and smooth.

Tim returned to his drink, "Leave me alone, Wes. I'm busy."

Westly Sweetooth took a seat next to Tim and smiled. "Busy nursing a beer?"

"Seemed like a good idea now that I'm fired."

"Don't you go all depressed-drunk on me, now. Let the rest of us catch up first."

Westly motioned to the bartender for a drink. Westly was strong and well-built with a dark complexion and darker eyes. His strength was well-documented. As a Head Hunter, he had earned his stripes as a top performer.

He looked at Tim. "Look, man, don't beat yourself up. So your stock didn't get picked up by the bigwigs. It happens. No sense moaning about it."

Tim stirred in his seat and rolled his eyes. "Easy for you to say, man. You've hit over two hundred percent of quota for two months back to back. It's been a bad year, Wes. I don't think I'm cut out for this job anymore."

"But the Barons need us. They need Hunters to go out and score bodies. You're essential to the place, man. Trust me, they need us bad."

"I've been with the company for eight years. I've seen Hunters come and go. And the ones who stay—They become...different. This job eats you alive if you let it."

Westly grinned. "Man, if I wanted to hear nothing but bitching and whining I would have gone home."

Tim looked at Westly. "Hey, be nice! Amanda is a wonderful woman. You're a lucky man."

"Yeah? Shit, then you marry her."

"Oh no no no! She's all yours, my friend. Besides, my commission check isn't big enough to satisfy a woman like that."

Westly laughed into his glass. "She *is* a woman of expensive tastes." He threw back a shot of something cheap and leaned toward Tim.

"Listen, I got a new job that came in a few minutes ago, just before I pulled up. Ordered straight from the top. I got first pick of the draw. And I get to tag anyone I want on the job with me. Triple the pay rate."

Tim said nothing, only stared at his pint glass.

"So I figured maybe you might want in on the action. Easy split fifty/fifty."

"How the hell is that gonna work? I'm about to get terminated."

"Let me handle the bigwigs, man. You don't have to worry about them."

There was a pause. The bartender slid two glasses in front of them.

Tim sighed. "What's the job?"

"Does that mean you're in?"

"I don't think I've got much choice."

Westly laughed and slapped Tim's back. "Meet me tomorrow." He pointed his index finger above his head. "I'll clear everything with the boys upstairs in the meantime."

***

The following day, Tim arrived early and sat on his motorbike above the hilltop watching the sun. The Barons had given him a performance reset, a clean slate. It was an opportunity to win back their favor and make up for past losses.

The bone-chilling wind hit his face. He reflected on his life and his eight years as a Hunter. The bodies he procured for the Barons, the families he had broken up, the lives he had sold for coin, all in the corporate interest, all for a cold beer and a warm bed.

From the hill, he looked at the junkheads aimlessly walking through the rundown city like zombies in a black-and-white picture show. They had nothing but the clothes on their back. They would scavenge for scraps of food through the garbage piles. Sometimes a dead dog would do.

He shook his head. He didn't want to think of it anymore.

From behind him came the distant humming of an engine.

Westly arrived, his rifle already perched and ready before he dismounted from his motorbike.

"You made it."

"Yeah." Tim frowned. "Why wouldn't I?"

"Nothing. Just a good sign is all."

Tim ignored the comment. "So who is the target?"

"Special order. This one comes with specifics."

"Fuck, of course it does."

"Lose the attitude! Listen up. This one hasn't gone company-wide yet. The Barons put in a special order based on some upcoming corporate changes that haven't been made public."

Tim's eyes narrowed. "Okay. What does that mean?"

"It means if everything goes well and you pull this off, the bigwigs will be indebted to you. You'll move on up. Be a part of the A players."

"Yeah fine. Let's get this over with already," Tim moved off and crouched into position.

Westly tapped his earpiece. "Target is on the move, man. Get ready."

Tim gripped the rifle gently and lined up the scope. "What am I looking for, Wes? You still haven't told me anything useful."

"Just keep your sights west on the main road."

Tim's breathing slowed, his finger on the trigger. The wind was dying down.

Westly tapped his earpiece. "Target approaching. Ten seconds."

"Wes, who is the target?"

"Keep your sights on the corner. Wait until I signal."

"Wes—"

"There!"

In the sight of his scope came a minivan preparing to park on the corner of an empty street. The driver, a woman, exited as the side door slid open. Two little girls leaped out of the van and grabbed their mother tightly, frantically searching their surroundings.

Tim looked up from his scope, his eyes locked on Westly.

"Take 'em, man. The girls."

Tim didn't respond. He looked through the scope one final time.

"What are you waiting for?"

Tim was silent.

"Do it!"

Tim stood up, shuffling away the dirt and pebbles. He headed towards his bike.

"Tim! Where are you going?"

"I'm done here." He didn't look back.

"Are you crazy? You're gonna walk? Just like that?"

"I'm not selling kids to work in factories. Find someone else."

Tim heard the cocking of a blaster. He stopped, then turned.

There was a loud pop.

Tim's stomach tightened, and a sharp sensation came over him. His body curled inward and he slumped to his side. The side of his face slapped against the puddle on the street. There was a tightness around his chest like his heart was looking for an escape route.

Westly holstered his blaster. "You're not dying. Non-lethal round."

Tim mumbled, "Wes...don't."

"Sorry, brother. It isn't personal."

Tim mumbled again, struggling to catch his breath, "Why?"

"You were right, man. This brutal life takes a bite out of you day after day, hunt after hunt. You and I have both seen people lose themselves in this profession."

Tim began to shiver. The effects of the stun kicked its way through his body.

Westly leaned over Tim. "But you know what I think? About all those people who walk through this life? All those who fell short, gave up, or were terminated?"

He stepped closer and whispered, "They're weak. Everyone thinks they can drive better than anyone. Everyone knows they're great in bed, right? Bullshit! It's the same with our profession. You think just anyone can rise to the top? That's not how it works at all, man.

"So many soft people crack at the first sign of pressure, or falter when they miss quota. They have a bad month and they let it eat at their core. So many people hate what they do for a living. Can you believe that? Me? Hell, I can't imagine doing anything else. This job is a privilege, Tim. Don't you understand that? The sleepless nights, the pressure of the job—it's all a privilege."

Wesley laughed and shook his head. "I thought you'd be different, man. I really did. I thought you just needed a kick in the ass to get into the proper mindset and you'd be one of us. I hate being wrong."

He turned his back and mounted his motorbike. "I'll be back for you later. Management arranged for your spot on the auction block if you didn't follow through today. Threw in the extra comp for the inconvenience."

Westly drove off, heading for the children, leaving Tim in the dust, cold and alone.

Tim couldn't speak. The foul air of trash all around him assaulted his nose. There was an incessant ringing in his ears. As he lay on the abandoned street, he glanced above him and reunited with the sun making its daily retreat that evening. The Surface Level was a grimy and soulless place to live, but you couldn't find a more immaculate sunset.

For once in his life, after eight years of running up and down between levels, after hustling his way through life by any means he could, and after failing to make his quota to appease the factory bosses, he found something that he hadn't realized he'd been searching for.

No more hunts. His body would be placed on the auction block and sold, but that didn't matter. None of it mattered anymore.

Somehow he wasn't afraid. Oddly enough, relief washed him clean. Despite his circumstances, he had found something that no amount of money or hustle was able to grant him.

For a moment, he found peace.

Grind

6:30 a.m.

For Mr. Kevin Anker, work was a pleasure that had no equal.

That morning, the sixty-one year old man breezed through the sea of empty, dull-looking cubicles. The automatic ceiling lights flashed on with each step he made.

When he arrived at his seat he snapped his briefcase open and fished for his company laptop. He popped it open. His fingers slammed against the keys.

What wonderful music, he thought as the *clicks* and *clacks* filled the office, transporting his mind to the work at hand. Glorious work.

What will I focus on today?

Department spreadsheets? Email cadences? Slides for the Quarterly Review? Perhaps he would reorganize the database records again? It didn't matter. Variety was not his style. That would be *inefficient*.

***

7:45 a.m.

The floor was piling up with other corporate drones now. The clicking was no longer sufficient to drown out the noise; the idle chitter-chatter that plagued him daily.

The youngins, the youths, and the graduates choked by their father's old neckties huddled near his desk and would recap "the game" from the night before, yacking endlessly.

Mr. Anker cleared his throat like a chain smoker hacking up something thick from below as a polite reminder that there was work to be done. He did this repeatedly until they cleared out.

He hadn't earned the title of manager yet. An oversight to be sure, but he had no interest in titles. He'd happily arrive early and stay late. He surrendered even his weekends to the humdrum of company projects.

The new offices occupied by Dressler, Duncan, Clark & Company, with their "open-concept" floor plan, bean bag chairs, a gaming room oddly busy during work hours, tiny glass telephone booths, and enough cold brew on tap to send your heart into overdrive earned his annoyance that Monday morning.

No doubt Dante would elect these office spaces as one of the circles of Hell. There was nothing wrong with the old offices. Nothing at all! The tall walls of the old cubicles ran high enough to make you feel secure at your desk, your own personal castle where you reigned as lord over your serfdom of files and billing reports.

Now Management opted for walls that barely reached your shoulder. You could actually *see* the person working next to you, in front of you, left, right and center. Mr. Anker groaned. Why change?

He knew why of course. The applicant pool was getting younger every day. Management had begun conceding efficiency and a productive work environment for the juvenile, dumb monkeys released from their overpriced colleges the previous Spring.

"Forward. Our company is always looking ahead," Mr. Duncan, the Managing Director, would say. He often responded with little quips he'd been collecting the over the decades. Enough maxims to produce a series of motivational posters you'd find plastered on walls in such a lackluster working office as this one.

Still, Mr. Anker's private thoughts and opinions would go to the grave with him. He would never dream of wasting time with petty office gossip.

He sat upright in his chair, tucked neatly at his white desk, and carried on.

***

12:09 p.m.

The floor emptied for the lunch hour. Though his stomach was rumbling on and off fifteen minutes prior, Mr. Anker pushed through, keeping his eyes focused, moving back and forth, back and forth from his dual monitors. With the exception of a few annoying bathroom breaks, the man was glued to his desk. The music of typing returned. He smiled.

Then he heard a succession of footsteps.

His fingers paused.

The walking continued with an incessant tapping of shoes on the thick vinyl floor.

He fixed his eyes on his watch. It was past noon.

Everyone should be at lunch. Who could still be on the floor?

The footsteps continued behind him, and the sound rang in his ears. Dear God, what if they came to his desk? He didn't dare look behind him. Eye contact would seal his fate forever.

Mr. Anker returned to his typing as best he could, but it was too late. The sound of the footsteps stopped at his desk. A pair of black shoes.

Ms. Debra Sun, from the one of the SMB sales teams, planted herself by his desk carrying two mugs filled and steaming with a dark roast she had brewed that afternoon. It was her ritual to say hello and bring over a drink. She couldn't help but be bubbly and friendly, a terrible affliction that troubled if not annoyed her seasoned coworker.

She young looking, possibly early thirties, with bright bluish-green eyes and golden hair held together in a ponytail. Her smile and upbeat personality would be regarded as infectious to a more receptive audience.

Mr. Anker glanced up at her, his fingers still swiftly flying across the keys.

"No lunch today?" Her voice ran a high octave that no woman, no matter how dainty, should be able to carry.

"No," Mr. Anker replied. "QBRs for Mr. Duncan are due in thirty minutes." He refused to look up at her or acknowledge the thoughtful gift of caffeine she placed on his desk in front of him. She leaned against his desk, trying not to pick at her green nail polish.

"You gotta take lunch," Debra said. "If you won't eat, at least stretch your legs outside. It's soooo nice out."

The typing continued in full force. It wasn't registering with her.

"Well, Kev, I'll let you get back to it. Some of us are starting the afternoon lunch walk and run this week. If you're interested—"

He squinted as he turned to her. "Thank you, but no." His blood ran cold at the childish nickname she had called him. He ceased typing and just stared.

She was beginning to understand. "Let me know if you change your mind." She turned and left him to his work.

A deep sigh escaped him. He looked at the time on one of the monitors: 12:15 p.m. He completed his report with fifteen minutes to spare and quietly took a sip from the mug next to him. Either way, he had to cease his typing for a moment. The joints in his hands felt as if they were on fire. The swelling and rubbing was getting more intense these days. He tried making an O shape with his thumb and the tip of his fingers, just like his OT suggested. Only a simple exercise, really.

His gaze wandered to a few of the other folks working around him. How these young, baby-faced boys with stubble cheeks sat at their desks, smiling and dialing away to prospective customers. Too foolish to realize the value of their youth.

Age was peering her grim, wrinkled face around the corner, her cold gaze seemingly fixed on the sixty-one year old. There was only so much he could do to try to repel her advances. His hair was thinning, the wrinkles on his forehead seemed to multiply each passing day, and his body was slower, ready to break at the first sign of pressure. Management reminded him occasionally of his senior rank, which felt more like a warning than a show of respect.

Could he keep up with the rising next generation?

He'd have to try.

As he took another sip from the coffee cup, the taste of burning sewage filled his mouth. *Decaf?* What a waste. He had gone to return the dreadful liquid to the kitchen in the back of the office when he heard his name called.

The voice was refined, sharp, and carried authority. "Kevin, do you have a moment?"

"Of course, Mr. Duncan."

"Excellent. My office when you're ready."

Mr. Anker dumped the coffee down the drain, placed the mug neatly in the dishwasher, and scurried off to his boss's plush corner office.

"Have a seat." Mr. Duncan's towering body looked awkward in his puny office chair. He was a silver fox, with a calm demeanor and large, powerful eyes. His hands were large too. If he clapped them together he'd send poor Mr. Anker's slight body flying across South Street Seaport.

Mr. Anker sat down in a chair in front of the desk.

"I've been watching you, Kevin. All of the management team has kept a close eye on you." Mr. Duncan reached to pull a file from his desk drawer, then continued. "You've done some of the best work on the floor. I should say *the* best."

Mr. Anker let a cheeky grin slip out as he twirled his thumbs over each other. It was rare to receive praise from Management, though he didn't doubt he deserved it.

"I'll get to it, Kevin." Mr. Duncan's voice shifted to being slow and deliberate.

Mr. Anker shifted in the chair and leaned forward, but only an inch or so. He didn't want to seem too interested.

"The business is looking to expand the Enterprise team. We'll need a new manager to lead it."

Mr. Anker's eyes widened with delight. He rubbed his thumbs until they were nearly raw. Finally.

"After reviewing your work last quarter, it only made sense to the Management team to—"

"Why, *me*?" Mr. Anker said with a not so subtle smirk. "I'm humbled, sir, really."

"Ask for your recommendation."

Mr. Anker frowned. "Come again?" His heart seemed to drop into his stomach and bounce around like a tennis ball.

"We'd like you to recommend someone. You are, after all, the most senior on your team."

The room, though opulent and spacious in the most executive way, suddenly shrank around Mr. Anker. He thought the temperature dropped, and the air soon became harder for him to breathe.

"A-a *recommendation*? You want me to—"

"Yes, management thinks it's only fair to ask a senior staff member such as yourself to submit a recommendation. It's a new policy I personally suggested." Mr. Duncan smiled that corporate smile, his teeth glistening white and bare, the skin tight around his mouth, his eyes absent of any light or color or charm. A corporate smile that he had perfected in his thirty-three years as Managing Partner. Every morning as he arrived at the office he admired his name on the company masthead.

Mr. Anker stood up. "No." His voice punched through Mr. Duncan's radiant, slimy smile.

"Pardon?"

"I'm sorry, Mr. Duncan, but I believe there isn't a single soul on the floor worthy of the title of manager."

"Oh." The old man recoiled back into his leather throne, his shoulders noticeably tensed.

"With all due respect, sir, I know the company's business better than anyone you employ. In the last quarter alone, I sold more telephone lines and computer services than anyone on the sales team. Look at my record, sir. You'll find not a single day of tardiness or sick time. Not one request for personal time off. Ever. I'm the first one in the office and the last to leave. With all that being said, I—"

"You make a compelling case, Kevin. I do recognize your contributions to the business, of course. But—"

Mr. Anker was frozen, hanging on every word.

"We are looking for fresh blood, someone we can train up. Someone—younger." He flashed his corporate smile again. "Kevin, think of this as a way to help bring up the next generation."

Next generation? The ones who take an additional twenty minutes on their lunch hour as if no one will notice? The generation that is far too timid to look you in the eye as you make your way to the bathroom? The generation that can't distinguish the difference between a stamp and a return label? *That* generation?

Mr. Anker blinked slowly as he eased back into his seat. He didn't dare argue with his boss. But he continued. "Chance."

"Pardon?"

"What if management simply gave me a chance to prove my worthiness of the position?" Mr. Anker knew his boss liked little competitions, challenges, spiffs, and opportunities to see his employees rise to special occasions.

Mr. Duncan's smile returned once more as his eyes almost sparkled. Almost. "I'm listening."

"Sir, allow me this chance to go above and beyond. You'll have no doubt in your mind about offering me the position! Not a single doubt."

His boss rose to his feet and stuck out his large hand to shake Mr. Anker's. "I like your attitude. I admire a man who is ambitious."

Mr. Anker's heart skipped a few beats when he clasped Mr. Duncan's hand in a sharp, firm grip. He had received the boss' blessing!

Now he just needed to find a way to make all this to work. Somehow.

***

For the first time in over thirty years, Mr. Anker took a lunch break.
Though it was unlike him and gave him an uneasy feeling in the pit
of his stomach, it was for good reason. A week later, he journeyed
downtown to Slater's United Medical Center. He remembered the
late-night commercials on TV and ads in the Sunday paper about the
new technical advances the Center had made. Slower bodies could be
made "new and vibrant again." He talked it over with his primary care
physician and his insurance company for the referral, then finally with
the chief of surgery at Slater, and he grew a little more confident in his
decision. But only a little.

He sat quietly in the empty waiting room of the center where it
seemed not a soul had ventured in years. The seats had dark stains,
the room was too tight and intimate, and the air was thick with the
smell of stale cigarette smoke desperate to break free from such dismal
surroundings. A television set was perched in the corner and stuck on
a static channel that served as white noise.

A green light flashed just above the door leading to the treatment
area and a harsh buzzer sounded. A pudgy old woman—the nurse,
in navy blue scrubs —came through the door. She fixed her gaze on
Mr. Anker. With too much eyeliner, her face carried a fierce scowl that
seemed to be held together with regret for the past decisions that had
led her life to this job. Like a ragged Miss Piggy puppet.

She said nothing, only gestured at Mr. Anker furiously, as if she had more patients waiting somewhere in a back room.

He leaped to his feet and followed the old pig puppet through the door and down the dingy hallway. A shabby carpet that stank of mildew and dead vermin. He covered his nose and pressed on.

The nurse opened the door to the examination room and pushed Mr. Anker inside. She motioned for him to sit on the table and quickly closed the door behind her. The lights flickered and the wallpaper was chipped. The room was stuck in the late 1970s, and Mr. Anker felt nauseated.

Was this a mistake? Perhaps I'm in over my head. Surgical alterations to the human body were a risky gamble, if not life threatening, even these days. What would it mean if he had parts of himself severed in exchange for certain medical enhancements? And all for a what? Company recognition?

But his work demanded he perform at his absolute best.

Am I willing to pay the price? Well, yes. This has to work.

He *needed* this to work. The position of management is a coveted prize. No other soul deserves such an honor, and none of them was fit to sharpen Mr. Anker's pencils.

Mr. Duncan himself had endorsed the notion of Mr. Anker's ascension to the position. And after all, he *was* the most senior. What were a few alterations, anyway? His insurance was good. That was all that mattered now.

There was a gentle rapping at the door.

Mr. Anker started.

Dr. Everett, in his surgical robes, came through the door and grinned. " Welcome back. "His face was oddly shaped like those of a chipmunk, plump and small, with excitable eyes.

"Have you given enough thought to the surgery, Mr. Anker? You understand, once the alterations have been made, there is no going back. Your original hands will be gone for good. The process cannot be reversed under any circumstances."

Mr. Anker looked down at his hands and then balled them into fists. "Yes, I understand. When do we begin?"

The doctor nodded and smiled

****

The surgery was successful and Dr. Everette was pleased with his work.

Kevin Anker was not going to rest any longer than he needed to. His eagerness to return to the office was palpable. A prescription of painkillers did what it needed to do for the time being.

The office floor hummed along with busy bodies at their desks. Another day filled with endless phone calls, morning stand-up meetings, and idle chatter about last night's mindless TV shows. Everyone was perfectly placed at their stations on a typical work day.

With his new prosthetic hands, Mr. Anker quickly went to work that morning. Long, thin bionic instruments protruded from the bone of his fingers. Mechanical ligaments and gears emitted a slight hiss every now and then. His arthritis was gone. His fingers could practically burn holes in his keyboard if he wasn't careful.

Though he already was lacking in coworker camaraderie, the sheer sight of his industrial hands—every now and then they oozed a vile grease and hummed like a motorized toy sports car—the other corporate drones made every effort to avoid him. There were rumors circulating through the office about him.

"Was he in an accident? Is this a weird, extreme attempt at dark humor?"

After witnessing his new upgrades, they feared to approach him. No one knew the real reason for the changes, of course, and Mr. Anker was delighted in his solitude.

Word spread so quickly that the HR department dispensed a company-wide memo instructing employees to respecting the rights of those who wished to go through permanent, albeit radical, medical changes to their anatomy.

The petty office gossip didn't stop him, but it invigorated him. At last he was free to continue to be a productivity machine with the help of his additions. He became more efficient by the day.

Many of the staff opted to work in single pods, and some moved their desks far away from him.

An added bonus, Anker thought. Then the music of his typing sent him back into a trance. This was the edge he needed. With no one to bother him with tedious small talk, he could increase his output and easily secure the promotion. The title of manager would be his in no time.

His typing speed increased, and the paperwork was filed within seconds. During lunch he'd skim Slater Medical Brochures wondering what other enhancements he could use. Pesky bathroom breaks? Try a steel catheter. Sleep getting in the way? Why not upgrade to an external electric battery?

So many choices. Soon his old body would be gone and his age would truly be a simple number.

Though many of his coworkers found it difficult to concentrate with the occasional grease stains on the floors as well as the loud mechanized motors running overtime, they hesitated to complain. His ears suddenly perked up when the sound of high heels grabbed his attention.

Debra Sun seemed to be the only person in the office not intimated by Mr. Anker's new hands. During the lunch hour, she placed a mug of something hot on his desk. She watched his bionic fingers clanking away, then smiled. "I thought you might want some coffee."

He paused for a moment, then turned his head to meet her gaze. He knew she felt uneasy about his prosthetics. Yet she still brought him a cup of coffee.

What was her angle? Was she making a play for the role of manager? Her?

He let the thought linger. How ridiculous! He entertained the idea of her running meetings, dispensing memos and "ways for him to improve" during annual performance reviews.

But he only smiled.

Debra pulled out a plastic straw from the pocket of her sweater and offered it to him. "I thought maybe you might need this. Make it easier to enjoy your coffee and all."

Mr. Anker reached up, the gears of his hands and fingers whining. His fingers curled slightly as he tried to grasp the straw.

Then the sounds came all at once. A sharp squelch and a wet crunch, soon accompanied by a shriek with enough force to shatter the windows of the whole office.

It took him a moment to fully realize the extent of what had happened.

Slowly he scanned his white desk. It was darkened by a small ruby pool containing three, maybe four, thin white fingers with dark green nail polish.

Mr. Anker's once clean blue shirt was sullied with large inky patches and blackened blotches.

Spots of blood also painted his face. He looked like an original Jackson Pollock painting. The screams of the young woman made him quiver at first, but soon he was motionless. He looked up at the sea of eyes of the many coworkers who stood in fear at the horror of the scene.

Debra Sun collapsed, still holding her mutilated right hand. A woman and two men rushed to help her.

An authoritative voice echoed across the office floor, "What's happened?" It was Mr. Duncan.

The people of the office kept their distance, murmuring to each other about what they had witnessed.

"Let me through!" Mr. Duncan pushed his way through the crowd and nearly gagged at the sight of Debra's fingers on the desk.

"Get an ambulance! Kevin?"

"I—This was an accident. I didn't—"

"Enough. Not another word." Mr. Duncan shook his head. No corporate smile this time. To someone, he yelled, "Get security up here. Now! This man must be removed immediately!"

Mr. Anker was alone and at the mercy of his boss and his peers.

As someone hauled Debra away, he looked at the titanium hand that had done the deed. A hand that was now coated with the blood of the only person who showed him any kindness. Someone who approached him with a smile and a hot drink every afternoon, who smiled at him and encouraged him to participate in company activities. She was a ray of sunshine in this cold, lifeless place.

Kevin Anker did not say another word, nor did he resist the security people when they came for him. They escorted him into the elevator

He said nothing, only wept. Neither his deep desire for recognition nor the most coveted title would ever be his.

A man with great ambition, but an aging body, had discovered that the price of continued career success was marred in blood. With his shiny, titanium claws being scrapped, Debra rushed to the ER, and his termination from the company, he became overwhelmed with the worst realization: He had finally been rendered—inefficient.

Special acknowledgment and a warm thank you to some truly special people in my life.

Many thanks to my wife, Michelle, for her love, encouragement, and for being a loving mother to our son.

Special thanks to Thomas J. Bevan for providing a wonderful online refuge known as "The Soaring Twenties Social Club," where I've met several writers, painters, musicians, filmmakers, comedians, soap makers, flaneurs, gourmands, gamblers, rogues, and overall good people, and encouraging many of us to pursue our craft and share it with the world. Most importantly, thank you Tom for helping me jumpstart my writing career.

Many thanks to Harvey Stanbrough, my writing mentor and the copyeditor of this manuscript.

To my brothers in Christ: Brady Putzke for being a brother, fellow student of the pulp writers, a good friend, and terrific storyteller. Zack Grafman, for his spiritual counsel, supreme taste in tobacco, his operational assistance with the P3 magazine and unrelenting optimism for the future. Jim Carran, for his support, Scottish wit, and bringing our little band of pulp writers together in the first place. Frank Kidd, for our mutual appreciation of John Milius movies, Max Brand yarns, and for being one of the first to really support (and naming) these Corpo Dread stories.

Glory to God for granting a boy a wild and vivid imagination that he could develop into a career as a storyteller.

"HIS NEED FOR HUNGER AND LOVE SATISFIED, MAN THEN SEEKS TO CREATE, BEING FASHIONED IN THE IMAGE OF GOD; AND IF HE CAN MAKE HIS CREATIVE WORK SUPPLY HIS NEEDS, IF HE CAN

MAKE HIS IMAGINATION PAY HIS BILLS, HE IS IN THE SEVENTH

HEAVEN."

H. BEDFORD-JONES

About the Author

Frank Theodat wrote his first story at the age of seven. Initially aspiring to be a screenwriter, Frank soon realized that a ballpoint pen and a legal pad were more cost-effective than film school. In 2020, he delved deep into the craft of fiction and has been dedicated to establishing himself as a professional pulp writer ever since. His penchant for unusual tales is inspired by classic TV anthologies such as Rod Serling's 'The Twilight Zone', and the literary works of Ray Bradbury, Charles Beaumont, Harlan Ellison, and Richard Matheson.

Currently, he pens short stories and maintains a newsletter, 'The Pulp Fictioneer', on Substack. This newsletter features flash fiction, craft book reviews, and articles that highlight the impact of pulp writers.

Outside of his writing endeavors, Frank is the Co-Founder and Editor of 'Pulp, Pipe, & Poetry Magazine': The variety magazine to elevate your leisure hours with fiction, verse, curation, & opinion. He has a fondness for old movies, vintage paperbacks, cigars, comic books, and spending time with his family. Frank lives in Southeast Massachusetts with his wife and son.

You can follow him on Twitter (@frank_theodat), sign up for his newsletter, 'The Pulp Fictioneer'.

www.ingramcontent.com/pod-product-compliance
Lightning Source LLC
Chambersburg PA
CBHW051249160726
47994CB00003B/1082